the MUSEUM

Museum open

BY SUSAN VERDE · ART BY PETER H. REYNOLDS

Abrams Books for Young Readers
New York

When I see
a work of art,
something
happens in
my heart.

I cannot stifle
my reaction.
My body just goes
into action.

This one makes me
want to pose
and stand up on
my tippy-toes.

Now I'm all twirly-whirly,

twinkly, sparkly, super swirly.

Whew!
Exhausted.

I take a breath.
I can't wait to see
what's next.

Hmmm... I think I'll analyze

the whos and whats and wheres and whys.

I'm starting to feel so
sad and blue—
heavy, lonely,
through and through.

I think I need
something to eat.
Those apples
would be such
a treat.

I'm skipping through a field of flowers.

I could keep this up for hours.

Fragrant, soft, and so delightful.

Suddenly, it's all so frightful!

I make silly faces
at a guy.
<u>He</u> did it first!

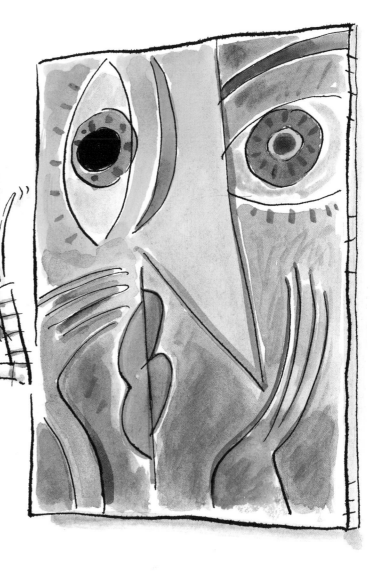

I do not lie!

I'm giddy from all these
lines and squiggles.
I collapse in fits of giggles.

Wait!

What is this I see?

An empty canvas stares at me.

Where is the color?
What does it mean?
It's the strangest art
I've ever seen.

Is this a joke?
I shut my eyes,
and something
happens, to my
surprise.

I start to see things
in my head,
yellow, blue, then green
and red,

circles, lines, all kinds of shapes,
faces, flowers, and landscapes.

I open my eyes
and look once more
at the canvas that
I saw before...

It's mine to fill
the way I choose,
a purple dot, a pair of shoes,
ZigZag lines, the deep
blue sea, a portrait
of my mom and me.

No longer blank,
it's my creation...

I am feeling such elation!

What a glorious time
I've had—I've been
scared, silly, mad,
and glad.

I'm energized from head to toe.

Even when it's time to go.

The museum's closed
for the night;
but I know that
it's alright.

Its rhythm exists
in all I see.
The museum lives
inside of me.

For my three muses, Joshua, Gabriel, and Sophia, who fill my heart
with endless joy, love, and inspiration.
—S.V.

To Emma Walton Hamilton for connecting the dots.
—P.H.R.

During a visit to a local art show in East Hampton, one of my children was looking at a still life painting of some fruit and suddenly became ravenous! In an attempt to distract him from his rumbling tummy, I began to create a poem about how each of the pieces of art around us made us feel. It was then that the idea for *The Museum* was born. It is my hope that this book will inspire children to notice how art makes them feel and ignite a desire to express themselves through their own creativity! —Susan Verde

What a joy to bring Susan Verde's words to life! The emotion in this book is exactly what fuels my own creative journey. It was fun to do my "ish-ful" nods to famous works of art and add a few of my own originals in along the way. I hope the spirit of this book inspires you to visit a museum, fill your own art gallery, or just savor the emotions that make life a rich journey. —Peter H. Reynolds

The illustrations in this book were created using watercolor.

Library of Congress Cataloging-in-Publication Data

Verde, Susan.
The Museum/written by Susan Verde; art by Peter H. Reynolds.
p.cm.
Summary: A young girl tours and twirls through museum galleries experiencing
different emotions evoked by different styles of art, and then expresses
her energy and inspiration when she finds an empty canvas.
ISBN 978-1-4197-0594-6
[1. Stories in rhyme. 2. Art appreciation—Fiction. 3. Art museums—Fiction.
4. Museums—Fiction.] I. Reynolds, Peter, 1961- ill II. Title.
PZ8.3.V712638Mus 2013
[E]—dc23
20120 22518

Text copyright © 2013 Susan Verde
Illustrations copyright © 2013 Peter H. Reynolds
Book design by Peter H. Reynolds and Chad W. Beckerman

Printed and bound in China
10 9 8 7 6 5 4 3 2 1

Abrams Books for Young Readers are available at special discounts when purchased in quantity for premiums and promotions as well as fundraising or educational use. Special editions can also be created to specification. For details, contact specialsales@abramsbooks.com or the address below.

ABRAMS
THE ART OF BOOKS SINCE 1949
115 West 18th Street
New York, NY 10011
www.abramsbooks.com